To Saskia and Hanna

KINGFISHER
An imprint of Larousse plc
Elsley House, 24-30 Great Titchfield Street,
London W1P 7AD

First published in 1995 by Kingfisher
2 4 6 8 10 9 7 5 3 1
Copyright © Kady MacDonald Denton 1995

A CIP catalogue record for this book
is available from the British Library

ISBN 1 85697 306 9

Designed by Chris Fraser
Colour separations by P & W Graphics, Singapore
Printed in Italy

Would They Love a Lion?

• *Kady MacDonald Denton* •

Kingfisher

Anna dreamed she was a bird.
But when she woke up, she wasn't.

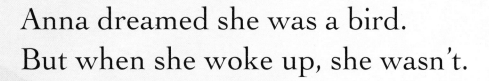

I could be a bird, said Anna. I could be.
And she flapped her wings.

I will be a bird.
And I'll have a nest.

A nest is too small, said Anna.
I want a cave. A big cave, a bear's cave.

I'll be a bear.

And Anna the bear growled
and went to breakfast.

A bear is too small,
said Anna.
No one notices a bear.
I'll be an elephant.

And Anna the elephant went outside
and thumped and swung her trunk.
But that isn't enough, said Anna.

I want to make the world shake.
I need to be bigger, really big, the biggest of all.
I'll be a huge . . .

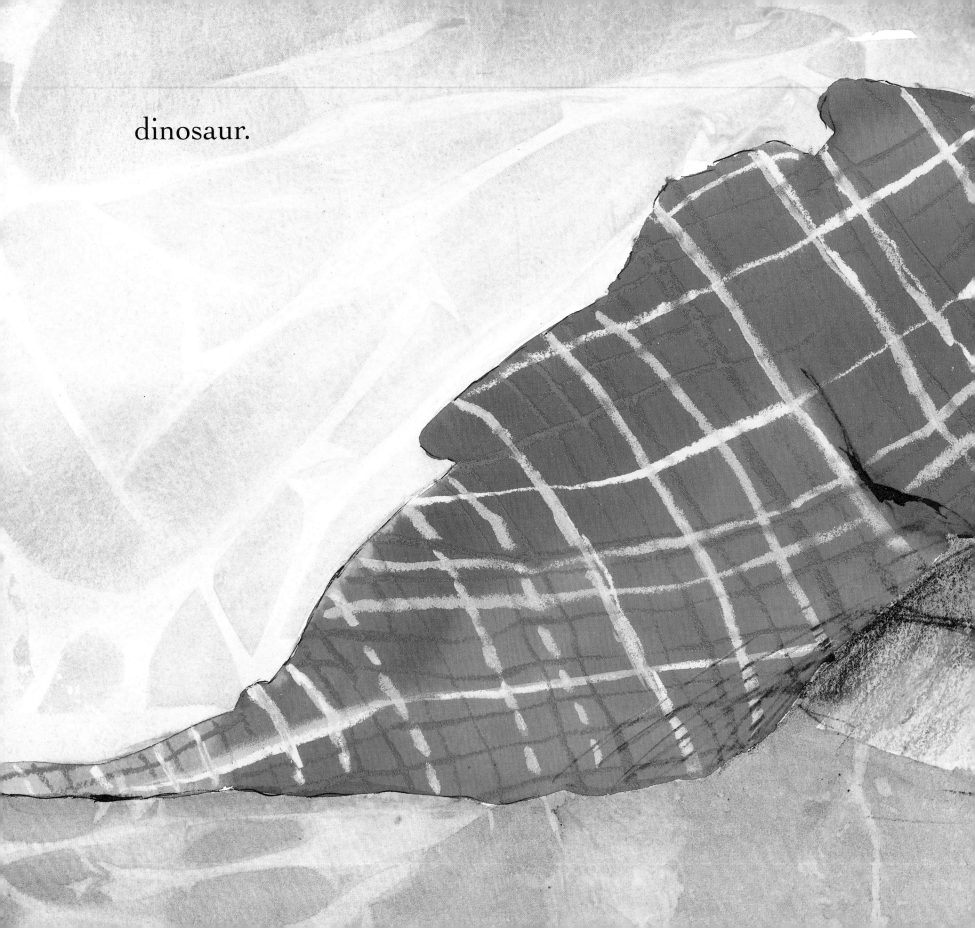

dinosaur.

That's big, said Anna.
But now I'm all alone.
You can't cuddle a dinosaur.

I could be a rabbit. Everyone loves a rabbit.
And Anna the rabbit stopped for a kiss.
That's nice, said Anna. But . . .

A rabbit is too quiet.
I don't want to be quiet.
I want to play games.
I'll be a kitten - a cat -

A lion!
A lion loves to play.
Would they love a lion?

A lion can hide and a lion can roar.

Lions stalk.
Lions pounce.

Lions eat fast.
Lions run fast.

But lions get tired and love to sleep.
Would they love a lion?
Yes, they'd all love a lion.

And Anna the lion settled in for a nap.